Is Seeing Believing?

AND OTHER MYSTERIES
Compiled by the Editors
of
Highlights for Children

BOYDS MILLS PRESS

Compilation and jacket illustration copyright © 1993
by Boyds Mills Press, Inc.
Contents copyright by Highlights for Children, Inc.
All rights reserved

Published by Boyds Mills Press, Inc.
A Highlights Company
815 Church Street
Honesdale, Pennsylvania 18431
Printed in the United States of America

Publisher Cataloging-in-Publication Data
Main entry under title.
    Is seeing believing? : and other mysteries / compiled by the editors of
Highlights for Children.
[96]p. : cm.
Stories originally published in Highlights for Children.
Summary: A collection of mystery stories.
ISBN 1-56397-192-5
1. Detective and mystery stories—Juvenile fiction.
[1. Detective and mystery stories.]
I. Highlights for Children. II. Title.
[F]   1993
Library of Congress Catalog Card Number: 92-73627

First edition, 1993
Book designed by Tim Gillner
The text of this book is set in 12-point Garamond.
Distributed by St. Martin's Press

10 9 8 7 6 5 4 3 2

Is Seeing Believing?

CONTENTS

Is Seeing Believing?

By Mike McCann

My best friend Billy had stayed for supper and, having hungrily emptied our plates, we quickly cleared the table. We were in a hurry to get back to our project.

"So, boys," said my father, "how is that clubhouse coming along?"

"It's almost finished, Dad," I answered. "May we be excused so we can work on it some more?"

"Sure," he agreed, "but only until dark!"

"And, Brian," Mom called out as we moved

toward the door, "when you're through at that clubhouse, I'd like you to go next door and introduce yourself to our new neighbors, the Franklins. Their daughter Jenny is about your age, and it would be nice if you tried to make her feel welcome."

"OK, Mom," I replied, not quite sure of what we would do with her, but I figured that one more friend wouldn't make our clubhouse any less of a special place.

Billy and I raced across my backyard. When we reached the ladder that rose to our treetop clubhouse, I grabbed my friend's sleeve to keep him from climbing up. "Say, Billy," I said, "why don't we invite Jenny over? Maybe if she pitches in, we'll finally finish this tree house!"

"Great," said Billy.

When we entered the Franklins' yard, we had to wade through the knee-high grass that hadn't been cut while the house was for sale. As we neared the front door, I noticed that the lights were on in the basement. "They may still be un-packing," I suggested. "We'd better take a look before we disturb them."

Billy and I knelt beside the small basement window, and what we saw inside nearly scared us to death! Mr. Franklin was turning the handle of a long green machine. Each time he did so, a shiny black roller spun with a clankety-clank as a large square of paper emerged from the side. It was . . . MONEY!

"They're counterfeiters!" I gasped. "Our new neighbors—they're counterfeiters!"

"Hi, guys! What's going on?"

Spinning around, we found a girl standing above us. Without a word, we ran right past her!

Back at our clubhouse, Billy looked at me fearfully. "What are we going to do, Brian?"

"I don't know," I replied.

"Should we tell our parents?"

"No. They might think we were just imagining."

"Well . . . what about the police?"

"No," I said as an idea came to mind. "Not without proof. So, here's what we'll do. . . ."

The next day at school I sat next to Billy in the lunchroom. "Did you get it?" I whispered.

Billy eased his backpack onto his lap. "Yes," he replied as he lifted the flap to reveal his mother's Polaroid camera tucked beside his notebooks. "Mom said we could borrow it if we pay for the film."

"That's OK," I said with a smile. "When we get the reward, we'll be able to buy her a whole new camera!"

Our laughter quickly ended when the same girl approached our table. "Hello again, guys," she said. "I'm Jenny Franklin. I saw you yesterday, remember? May I sit here?"

"Errr . . . yes," I answered nervously as I stood up with my tray. "Go right ahead. We were . . . just leaving." Billy followed me to another table. I felt terrible inside.

Later that evening, we crawled through the grass like snakes as we carefully moved toward the Franklins' basement window. I was scared, yet kind of glad, to find Mr. Franklin printing even more counterfeit money! I aimed the camera through the dirty window glass. "Get ready to run," I hissed.

When I pressed the button, the flash reflected into our eyes and, for a moment, Billy and I were blinded. As my eyes began to clear, I grabbed my best friend's arm. "Let's move!" I yelled as I pulled him to his feet.

As we were running away, I heard a screen door open. "Hey, you boys! Wait a minute!" The loud, harsh voice was surely Mr. Franklin's. We certainly didn't wait.

When we got back to the clubhouse, we placed our "evidence" on the floor between us. As dark-ened blobs began to form on the photo, we heard someone begin to climb our ladder! Billy grasped my arm, and he held so tightly that it really be-gan to hurt!

I was sure relieved when Jenny Franklin—not her father—appeared in our clubhouse hatchway. "I know you guys don't want to play with me," she said. "But I want to give you this anyway, because we're neighbors."

Jenny placed a rectangular box before us. "It's a game called Bargain Hunt," she continued, lifting the lid. "My parents make it at home, in our basement. It's a lot of fun. I hope you like it."

When Billy and I saw the real-looking play money tucked inside that box, we knew right away that we'd made an awful mistake!

"Jenny!" I called.

"Yes?"

"Do you think you could explain Bargain Hunt to us and maybe stay and play for a while?"

Jenny smiled brightly. "Why sure!" she agreed as she climbed up into our hideaway. "Basically, you move your piece around the board and purchase the most valuable items you find. Only, some things look expensive, but are really kind of junky. Other things seem worthless, but turn out to be old and quite costly. So you can't make your decisions just by the way things *look*. Understand, guys?"

Billy and I smiled broadly. "Yes, Jenny," I said. "Thanks to you . . . we understand!"

The Mysterious Cat Lady

By Marilyn Kratz

"Look, Nancy," said Jill. "Only one can of peanuts left."

"Good. We've made a lot of money for our baseball team," said Nancy.

"Coach Miller said we have to sell *all* of them to get enough money for those new uniforms," Jill reminded Nancy. "Come on. There's just one house left on the street."

"But you know whose house that is," said Nancy, plopping down in the grass along the curb.

"Sure, it's where the Cat Lady lives," said Jill. "You don't believe all those stories about her, do you?"

"Well . . ." Nancy tossed a ragged old baseball from hand to hand. "All I know is that Freckles Severson used to go to her house all the time and suddenly he disappeared."

"He probably just moved away," said Jill.

"Then how do you explain that big white cat with brown spots like freckles that showed up around the Cat Lady's house?" demanded Nancy.

"Come on, Nancy," scoffed Jill. "Nobody can turn a boy into a cat. You've been watching too many science fiction shows on TV." She picked up the box with the last can of peanuts. "Come on, scaredy CAT!"

"Big joke!" muttered Nancy, following Jill down the street.

A sagging wire fence overgrown with vines surrounded the Cat Lady's old house. Jill unhooked the low gate, and the girls stepped into the shady yard.

"Better close this gate," said Jill. "We don't want any of her cats to get away."

"I don't see any cats," whispered Nancy.

"She probably keeps them in the house," said Jill. "Come on." She stepped up to the door. Finding no doorbell, she knocked softly.

"Remember, we won't go inside her house, no

matter what!" Nancy whispered.

The girls heard footsteps. Then the door opened just a crack.

"Yes?" said a soft voice.

"Uh . . . we . . . we're selling peanuts," Jill began nervously. Then she remembered Coach Miller's selling instructions, and she started over.

"Good afternoon, ma'am," she said. "My name is Jill Burns, and this is Nancy Johnson. We're selling peanuts to earn money for uniforms for our baseball team. We have just one—"

"Come in quickly!" the voice said. The door opened a little wider, and an arm swept the girls inside before they realized what had happened.

"Hey!" Nancy protested weakly as the door was closed quickly behind them.

It took a minute for Jill's eyes to adjust to the dimness inside the house. When they did, she saw that they were standing in a small living room filled with overstuffed furniture. Pictures of cats were everywhere, and sitting here and there were several real cats.

"I didn't mean to startle you," said the woman. Her blue eyes twinkled. "But I didn't want any of my cats to get out, you see." She motioned to the sofa. "Won't you sit down?"

She settled herself in a chair. Immediately, three cats jumped onto her lap.

"The peanuts are one dollar a can," said Jill.

She and Nancy remained standing near the door.

"I love peanuts," said the Cat Lady. "Now just wait here. I'll get a dollar." She brushed two cats to the floor and carried one with her into the next room.

Suddenly Nancy gasped and grabbed Jill's arm. She pointed to a photograph on a small table. "Look!" she whispered. It was a picture of Freckles Severson!

Just then a big white cat with brown spots sauntered into the room. It brushed against their legs, purring.

"Let's get out of here!" croaked Nancy.

But before Jill could move, the Cat Lady returned.

"Here's your dollar," she said. "Now don't rush off, girls. I think you can help me with a little problem I have."

"We really can't stay . . . ," Nancy began.

"It won't take long," said the Cat Lady, pushing the girls gently toward a doorway. She pulled aside an old brown blanket hanging over the doorway. Behind it was a stairway. "I have something special to show you."

"But, but . . . ," Nancy sputtered as the Cat Lady urged them up the stairs into a large, almost empty room.

"Wait here," she said.

Jill could feel Nancy's fingers digging into her arm as the old woman opened a closet door and pulled out a basket. Immediately, a big calico cat bounded out of the dark closet.

"Now, don't fuss, Whiskers," said the Cat Lady. "I just want to show the girls your babies."

She carried the basket over to the girls. In it were three tiny kittens, crying with weak little mews.

"Hey! They're real beauties!" exclaimed Nancy.

"Aren't they just!" agreed the Cat Lady. "I hate to give them up, but I already have more cats than I can care for now that my nephew, Donald Severson, has moved away."

"Donald Severson?" said Jill. "Do you mean Freckles Severson?"

"Oh, yes." The Cat Lady laughed. "I did hear his friends call him that. Yes, he was such a help."

"So Freckles moved away," said Jill, smiling at Nancy.

"Anyway," the woman went on, "I was wondering if you knew anyone who needs a good cat. I must give these away as soon as they can leave their mother."

"I'm sure we can find some people who'd like a cat," said Jill.

"I'd like one myself," said Nancy, gently rubbing one soft little kitten. "Of course, I'll have to ask Mom and Dad first."

"Oh, good," said the Cat Lady. "I'm sure you would take good care of a cat."

Just then the big white freckled cat bounded up the stairs.

"Hello, Freckles," the woman greeted the cat. Then she turned to the girls. "Freckles here was Donald's favorite cat." She smiled. "I'm sure you can see why."

Jill grinned at Nancy. "We sure can!" she said. And they all laughed together.

The Case
of the
Golden
Opportunity

By William and Loretta Marshall

Friday, Sept. 10

Today the most exciting thing happened since I started keeping this journal. I just got home from playing football when Mom said I had a letter. I never get letters, and here was a real handwritten letter addressed right to Mr. Jack Huff! Actually, my name is John Ryan Huff, Jr., but everyone calls my dad (John, Sr.) John, and they call me Jack. Anyway, there was this letter addressed to me. Here it is:

Dear Jack,

I'm a friend of Michael's and have just seen him this past weekend at the gold diggings in Alaska. When he heard I had a stopover here, he asked me to deliver a message to you. You weren't home when I called, so I'm sending this letter. He wants you to wire him $2,000 by Monday. He has a chance to buy an interest in the claim—says you won't regret it—you'll all get rich. But he has to have $2,000 by Monday. Send it by wire to Fairbanks. Your sister Eva will pick it up there.

Sincerely,
Tim

When I read the letter, I got all excited about getting rich and everything until I ~~remmembered~~ remembered that I don't know anyone named Michael, except the little boy next door, and I don't have a sister named Eva. I don't have any sister. Besides, I don't have $2,000. Actually, it has taken me two years to save $23.56, and I need at least another $5.00 before I can buy the electronic football game I want. If I had $2,000, I would be super rich! If I were rich, I would go to a real Broncos football game. I guess the letter really wasn't to me after all but to some grown-up Jack

Huff with $2,000 and a sister named Eva.

I feel sorry for Michael out there in the diggings waiting for the money. If I had it, I'd send it to him, but I don't even know his address.

Saturday, Sept. 11

All night I kept worrying about Michael and Eva and the other Jack Huff missing out on their big chance on the gold mine. So I got up real early and looked over the letter for clues. There isn't an address or whole name, except mine, on the letter anywhere.

I inspected the stamp ~~espeshully~~ especially because I saw this movie on TV where the stamp solved the whole thing. But this was just a plain old stamp. I looked at the postmark, and it was mailed on Thursday, right here in Denver. The way I figure it is that Michael and Eva are married, and this friend of Michael's named Tim flew here from Alaska and mailed me this letter by mistake because he looked up Jack Huff in the phone book, and my dad is the only John Huff in the book. (I know because I looked it up to see and there's no other John, Jack, or J. But there are about a zillion other Huffs—two whole ~~colloms~~ columns of them.)

When the mail carrier came, I asked her what the Post Office would do with the letter, and she said it would go to the dead-letter office. That's not going to help Michael or Jack at all.

So I decided it was up to me. After all, I'm the one who got the letter. First, I tried to find Tim. I called the airport and asked if any passengers named Tim had come from Fairbanks, Alaska, on Thursday. They said even if I knew his last name that was ~~confidenshull~~ confidential information. Besides, there aren't any flights directly from Fairbanks, and Tim might have been on any one of about a zillion flights because Stapleton Airport is the seventh busiest in the whole world. So I thought I'd better forget about finding Tim.

I thought about trying to call Michael and Eva in Alaska, but if they had a phone, they probably would have called Jack themselves. Besides, I don't know their last name or where they live in Alaska—and Alaska is BIG. (I know because I looked it up in an atlas.) You can't very well call up a state that has more than 591,000 square miles and more than 551,000 people and ask to talk to Michael!

So I decided to concentrate on finding Jack— at least he's right here in Denver somewhere. After lunch I started calling every one of the zillion Huffs (except the four who are my uncles and cousins) and asking for Jack and if they knew someone named Michael in Alaska. I was surprised at how huffy some Huffs can get! Hee-hee. I'm only about halfway through, but Mom said I have to go to bed anyway. I'll call tomorrow.

Sunday, Sept. 12

First thing in the morning I started calling, but after the third person yelled at me for waking him up at dawn on Sunday, I decided to wait awhile.

After church I called Huffs all day long, but no one I talked to knew Jack or Michael in Alaska. One lady I called said of course she knew Jack Huff, but she always watched old movies instead and she never listened to Alaskan stations. I think she was a little mixed-up, but she did thank me for calling. Maybe I'll call her again sometime. Well, as I was saying, I called Huffs all day, except, of course, during the Broncos game. My dad and I always watch the game together, and I'm sure Jack and Michael would understand.

Besides, I didn't want anyone else to yell at me. No one did, but no one knew Jack or Michael either.

So here I am at 9:00 on Sunday night, and I'm no closer to helping them than when I started. I feel terrible. Dad says I did all I could, and that was good enough. Too bad, enough wasn't enough to find a Huff.

THAT'S IT!!! Enough-Hough!

It was right there in the phone book—Jack M. Hough. I called and it was Michael's brother-in-law. He was so happy that I called, and when I told him how I had been calling all the zillion Huffs for two days (except during the Broncos game), he thanked me a lot and said that he and Michael (Scott is his last name) would always be grateful that they hadn't missed their golden opportunity. I feel great.

Friday, Sept. 17

I can't believe it! Jack Hough called tonight and asked if Dad and I would like to go to the Broncos game on Sunday with him. Would we! Tim's letter turned out to be my golden opportunity, too.

The Mysterious Visitor

By Susan Rowan Masters

I'd been at Ashville Elementary School exactly one week when it happened. I had asked Miss Quigly, my fifth-grade teacher, if I could stay to finish watering the plants.

"Well, all right," she said, "but don't be late for the assembly." After everyone else had lined up, she turned to me. "I'll expect you in the auditorium in four minutes, Shirley. When you leave, be *sure* you close the door tightly so it will lock."

"Yes, Miss Quigly," I answered. I had to fill the watering can twice just to water the large, potted schefflera. After replacing the can, I closed the door hard enough for the lock to click.

When I sat down in the auditorium, Preston's Magical Show had already begun. The magician was putting a mouse and pairs of doves, rabbits, and canaries into separate cages. He had made them appear under a red scarf.

At the close of the show we returned to our room. I was heading for my seat when I heard Allison let out a big whoop. "Hey, who poked holes in my papier-mâché?" she demanded.

We had finished our papier-mâché animals in art class the day before. Allison's elephant had been chosen to be in the Ashville School Art Exhibit the following Friday. Allison was so proud she kept her elephant on top of her desk. "It was perfectly all right before—" She stopped and spun to face me. "The door was locked when we got back, and you were in here before—alone." Glowering at me, she added, "*You* poked holes in my papier-mâché. That's why you were late!"

"I didn't do anything except water the plants. Honest!"

"It *had* to be you!"

Miss Quigly ended our squabble by sending us back to our seats. My cheeks felt hot and damp as I hurried to my place. I was beginning to wish I was back at my old school again.

By fifth period my classwork wasn't finished. Even though I usually like games, I was glad to miss recess. As everyone filed out, I stared at page 79 in my math book.

"Stay in your seat while I'm gone, Shirley," ordered Miss Quigly. I listened to nineteen pairs of sneakers parading down the hall.

Sighing deeply, I set to work on the multiplication problems. I was just finishing the last one when I stopped to stretch. Suddenly I heard pittering sounds from the back of the room. Scampering across the tile floor was a white mouse! He paused beside Allison's chair and then climbed up the sleeve of a sweater slung over the back of the chair. At the top, he jumped onto Allison's desk and poked his nose into the air. But the desk was bare.

"Aha," I said. "Returning to the scene of the crime." Quietly, I crept near him. When I was three feet away, the mouse jumped to the floor and took off.

"Hey," I yelled, "you can't disappear on me now!" But before I had a chance to catch him, he scrunched under the bookcase.

I was on my hands and knees when I noticed a pair of black oxfords beside me. I peered up at Mr. Harmon, the school principal. "Ah . . . hello, Mr. Harmon." I wasn't about to get up. If the mouse made a break for it, I had to be ready.

"There's a mouse under there," I explained, pointing. "A white mouse."

"Hummm . . . is that so?" said Mr. Harmon, lowering his head to eye the space below the cabinet. "I see him now," he whispered, craning his neck.

We were peering at two bright eyes when the door flew open. In came Miss Quigly, with the class trailing behind her. When she noticed Mr. Harmon and me, her mouth dropped open. Sud-denly the mouse ran toward the door. Miss Quigly spun around to dash out, but nineteen kids blocked the doorway.

This is my only chance, I decided, picking up the wastepaper basket. I dumped the papers on the floor and sprinted toward the mouse. Before he could sneak out, I plopped the basket down over him. A great roar went up as everyone clapped and cheered.

Mr. Harmon sent the custodian to fetch a small cage and explained what had happened. "Mr. Preston of Preston's Magical Show informed me earlier that one of his two white mice had escaped while he was busy setting up his props. It seems the mouse hid here in your room— until Shirley captured him."

After Mr. Harmon left with the mouse secured in a cage, Allison came back and stood beside my desk. Ignoring her, I kept busy checking over my math.

"I . . . I guess that mouse must've chewed up

my papier-mâché," Allison began. "I'm sorry I accused you."

Glancing up, I answered, "It's OK. Too bad about your elephant. It was really nice."

"So was your turtle."

"Turtle?" I started to giggle. "It was supposed to be a rhinoceros."

We laughed until Miss Quigly told us to "be quiet back there."

I had a feeling Allison was going to be my first real friend at Ashville School.

The Day Niagara Didn't Fall

By Lois Garbig Smith

Jed Morgan stretched himself to his full height and breathed deeply, trying to pull into himself all of the sparkly afternoon he could possibly hold. It was March 29, 1848. Spring would soon be here, and after the long hard New York winter, it couldn't come too soon to suit Jed. Beneath his feet the soil was still muddy and moist from yesterday's shower. His steps made little slip-slapping sounds as he jumped and hopped along the winding path which led from his father's farm down to the Falls.

Suddenly he stopped. Something was amiss. Something that he couldn't quite lay his finger on. What could it be? He listened. How quiet the air had become. That was it! It was too quiet.

Like all folks who lived along the river, Jed was accustomed to the roar of mighty Niagara Falls as it raged on and on, never stopping. Many nights he had been lulled to sleep by its distant thunder. Jed stood stock still, hardly believing what his ears did not hear. Could it be? He began to run.

At the edge of the chasm he looked down in amazement. The riverbed was empty. Only a few small puddles remained as evidence of the vanished torrent. Rocks which had been washed and rewashed for century upon century were becoming dry.

"Glory be!" Jed exclaimed. "How can this have happened?" He turned and raced for home.

"Pa, Pa," he called as he flew up the path. "Pa, the Falls is dry! There is no water in the river."

Pa Morgan looked up from the wagon wheel he was repairing. "What's that you say? Calm yourself, son. Don't josh."

"I'm not joshing," Jed panted. "It's true. The Niagara has run dry. Just listen."

Pa cocked his head to one side. His eyes

widened. "It can't be!" he exclaimed. Dropping his tools, he rushed toward the house. "Ma, Molly, light the lanterns," he shouted. "Come on! Something terrible has happened. Jed says the Falls is dry."

Darkness fell as the Morgan family hustled down the path to the Falls. Yellow lantern lights winked all up and down both sides of the gorge as other folks, aware of the strange silence, came to investigate.

Standing on the bank of the drying river, Molly spoke in a whisper. "Ma," she said, "I'm afraid."

Mrs. Morgan gathered her close. "Hush, dear, I'm sure everything will be all right." But the quiver in her voice told Jed that she did not really believe her own words. Other folks, too, not sure of what they were viewing, whispered their fears one to another.

As the night wore on, the crowd along the Niagara grew larger. Morning brought more and more sightseers, and by noon five thousand onlookers were camped near the silent Falls.

With bright sunshine overhead, the feeling of disaster lightened to one of near-gaiety. Jed and Mr. Morgan, joined by some of the more venturesome spectators, climbed down steep paths to walk among the rocks on the river bed.

"Look, Pa," Jed shouted, holding an arrowhead that he had spotted. "And here's another."

Soon the riverbed was alive with souvenir hunters searching for articles that countless Indians, generations before, had perhaps tossed into the rapids.

"Bravo! Hurrah!" Folks along the riverbank cheered a cavalry patrol which arrived and rode their horses down into the river valley, crossing to the other side. This was the only time in history that horsemen had defied Niagara and lived to tell the tale.

But with sunset the fear returned. Jed and his family joined hundreds of nervous folks who flocked to church services to pray for deliverance from the menace of the missing Falls.

Later, Jed tossed and turned in his bed, listening, listening, listening for the sound that would permit him to sleep peacefully.

With the approach of morning, Jed dropped off into a troubled sleep, only to be aroused by a faint trickling sound. "It's beginning to rain," he told himself. But the sound grew louder, more persistent, finally becoming a steady roar.

"Pa," Jed shouted, "Pa, wake up! Listen! The Falls is back."

Once again the Morgan family lit lanterns and hurried to the gorge. Sure enough. The Falls had returned in all its fury.

"Glory hallelujah," Pa shouted.

"Thank the Lord," Ma gasped.

It wasn't until months later that the Morgan

family learned what had actually happened. A peddler came by and cleared up the mystery.

"Well, you know," he said, "the Niagara River flows from Lake Erie northward into Lake Ontario. On the night the Falls stopped, there was a high wind blowing over Lake Erie. The force of it broke up the ice cover and pushed tons and tons of ice up into the headwaters of the Niagara.

"It piled up into a gigantic dam," he continued. "And that dam was so high and so strong that it just naturally stopped all the water that normally flows down the river and makes the Falls.

"That ice held back the water for almost two days," the peddler explained, "before it finally broke loose and moved on. With the ice gone, the Niagara could flow again. Sure was a sight to see—all that ice piled up across that river!"

"The Falls without any water made a strange sight to see, too," Jed said. Then a laughing thought struck him. "When Mother Nature decides to play an early April Fool's joke," he chuckled, "she certainly picks a good one."

Dan's Treasure

By Lida Smith

High in the branches of his lookout tree, Dan lazily watched the scene below. A car rolling along the winding road in the distance looked like a glistening green bug. He wondered why it stopped suddenly at a point close to the river. In a half-interested way, he watched as a man got out, opened the trunk, and took out a large box. It must be a heavy box, Dan decided, because the man seemed to have some trouble carrying it. Then he went back to the car and got a shovel. The man was soon going through all the motions of digging, first looking up and down as if to make sure he was not being watched.

Dan was very curious now. What was in the box? Why was the man burying it? And why was he afraid someone would see him?

Dan snapped his fingers. "I know, it's some loot. Probably a burglary committed pretty far from here."

He got himself into a more comfortable position. As he watched, his thoughts were flying. First he must check on this buried box and find out exactly what it contained. Then he would go to the police, maybe even the FBI.

He could see it all now. The *Morning Star* would read: LOCAL BOY UNCOVERS THOUSANDS. CLUE LEADS TO ARREST OF CRIMINAL. His picture would be on the front page. And all his friends—Pete, Joe, Gene, Smitty—would think he was a real hero.

Now the man had finished his job and was hurrying back to his car.

Dan quickly slid down the tree. He plopped down on the grass and, chin in hand, made his plans.

First of all, it would be better to have someone he trusted to help him. That was a heavy box. Pete was the boy. He was strong and he was Dan's best friend.

With his mind made up, Dan rushed into action.

He ran toward Pete's house to catch him before he joined the other boys. Luck was with him. Pete was just coming to the door.

"What's up?" Pete asked.

"Plenty!" said Dan. "Come around back of the barn, where we can talk."

"Well?" asked Pete, when they had settled themselves.

"Well . . . ," said Dan slowly, enjoying every minute. "First of all, you've got to promise to keep a secret. Can you?"

"You know I can," said Pete. "Remember the time you got an F on your math paper? I didn't say a word to—"

"Never mind that," said Dan. "Listen—"

Pete's mouth dropped open as Dan explained. "What are we going to do?"

"Well," said Dan, after some thought, "we can't dig it up now. There'll be a lot of traffic on that road this time of day."

"You're right," agreed Pete.

"Tomorrow morning would be the time." Dan stood up. "I'll have to check on the things we'll need—shovel, wagon, and something to break open the lock."

"Boy!" said Pete. "You sure think of everything."

"You have to think of everything," said Dan. "Now remember, not a word of this to anyone."

"OK," said Pete. He started off but called back,

"Will you be at the clubhouse for the meeting? It's in an hour."

"I'll be there."

For the next half hour, Dan busied himself with his preparations. Everything was in order when he left for the club meeting. As he walked down the road, his heart thumped with excitement.

He was the first one to arrive at the little shack they called their clubhouse, but he did not have long to wait till Pete arrived.

"Did you get everything ready?" asked Pete in a hoarse whisper.

"Sh!" cautioned Dan. "Not here!"

Joe burst through the doorway. "Wow, Dan, that's great about that buried loot!"

Dan turned and stared. "Pete, you—"

"Don't be sore," said Pete. "I didn't mean to tell. I met Gene on the way home, and he said, 'What's new?' And I accidentally told him."

"Pete—!"

"Wait a minute, Dan," Pete interrupted. "If you didn't want anybody to know, you shouldn't have told me." He turned toward Gene. "But, Gene, you promised you wouldn't tell."

"I only told Smitty!"

"And Smitty told Joe," said Dan. "OK, so you're all in on it. Here's what we have to do."

No school morning could have brought Dan out of bed so early. It was barely sunup the next day when he met the guys at the spot where the treasure was buried.

"It was right here, next to this clump of bushes," said Dan.

The boys took turns digging, and in a few moments the mysterious box was in view.

"It's only a cardboard carton," moaned Pete.

"Never mind," said Dan. "Help me get it out."

Dirt flew in their faces as they pulled open the carton. Then the excitement died in disappointment.

"Junk!" Dan kicked the box in disgust. "Why do you think he would have looked up and down as if he were afraid of being seen?"

"Maybe because of that." Smitty nodded toward a sign, NO DUMPING.

"Hey, look at this stuff," said Pete, who was digging around in the box. "Look at all these hinges. We could sure use them on our clubhouse door, couldn't we?"

All hands pawed through the box.

"Look at this nice piece of plastic," said Dan, drawing it out carefully.

"We could fix our window with that!" exclaimed Gene.

"Here's a bolt lock. Wouldn't that look great on our clubhouse door?" said Smitty.

"Say, there are all kinds of good stuff in here!" exclaimed Pete. "Let's take it over to the clubhouse."

41

They tied the box to the wagon and filled the hole with dirt.

"Let's go," said Dan.

"You sure *did* find a treasure, Dan," said Pete.

The Case of . . . the Missing Skateboard

By Jeanne Iacono Martin

It was on the first day of summer vacation that Tracy Fletcher opened her own detective agency.

In one corner of the family garage Tracy had arranged a card table and two chairs. On the table were a notebook and several pens. Next to the table was an old file cabinet. It was empty but Tracy believed it gave her office a business-like feeling.

Outside the garage Tracy hung her sign:

Tracy Fletcher Detective Agency
No Case Too Small

Around noon Angie Tom came into the garage. She was only ten years old, but she had earned the reputation of being the best skateboarder on the block.

"He took it," Angie said, and she flopped into a chair.

Tracy grabbed her notebook and a pen. "Took what?" she asked.

"My skateboard, of course," said Angie.

Tracy opened her notebook and wrote *Stolen —Angie's Skateboard.* "Describe your skateboard," she said.

"You've seen it!"

"I know," said Tracy, "but a complete description of a stolen object is important to a detective."

"Well, it's brown and has black grip tape," said Angie. "And David Stellino took it."

"What makes you suspect David?" asked Tracy.

"Because there is a contest at Skateboard World tomorrow. If I don't show, David will win for sure."

"Did you see David take it?"

"No, but he must have."

Tracy wrote *Suspect—David Stellino.* "I'll get right on it," she said.

"I hope you get my skateboard back before the contest," said Angie. "The winner gets a new ten-speed bike, and I sure want it."

Tracy went first to the Stellino house to question David. Mrs. Stellino answered the door.

"Hello," said Tracy. "I want to ask David if he will be entering the skateboard contest tomorrow."

"I'm afraid not," said Mrs. Stellino. "David has the chicken pox. He's been home sick for two days."

"I'm sorry to hear that," Tracy said.

Tracy walked straight down the street to Angie's house. Before she knocked, she wrote in her notebook *Suspect home with chicken pox.*

Angie and her German shepherd, Prince, came to the door. "Where's my skateboard?" asked Angie.

"Wooof!" said Prince.

Tracy patted Prince on the head. "David didn't take it. He's home with the chicken pox. This is a real mystery. Where did you last put your skateboard? There should be some clues at the scene of the crime."

Angie led Tracy to her bedroom. "There—in the corner," she said.

Tracy was a good detective. Soon she announced: "Clue number one. Here's a long brown scratch that runs down the wall."

Angie looked. "I'm sure I didn't do that."

"Probably the thief," said Tracy. "It looks as though someone grabbed the bottom end of the skateboard and it slipped right down, scratching the wall. Did you hear any strange noises?"

"Nothing."

Tracy wrote in her notebook *Clue #1—Long brown scratch.*

Then Tracy picked something up from the floor and handed it to Angie.

"Grass," said Angie. "It could have come from anyone's shoes. Doesn't prove a thing."

"Don't get discouraged," said Tracy. "You have a real good detective working on your case." She wrote *Clue #2—Grass.*

Angie smiled and said, "Stay for dinner."

During dinner Tracy questioned Angie more. "Was your skateboard in the corner after breakfast?"

"Yes," said Angie.

"What did you do after breakfast?"

"I wrote a letter at my desk."

"Then?"

"I took a bath. Ooooh!" squealed Angie. "It was right after my bath that I noticed my skateboard was gone."

Tracy opened her notebook and wrote *Skateboard missing after bath.* "Now we are getting somewhere," she said. "Pinpointing the time of the crime is important in solving a case."

Tracy looked out the window. Prince was rolling in the grass. She had an idea. "I want to look for more clues," she said.

In Angie's bedroom Tracy knelt down and looked closely at the floor. "Nothing more," she said. But as she was getting up she noticed something on the bottom edge of Angie's bedspread. She picked it off. Then another. And another. She wrote *Clue #3—Dog hairs*. "I think Prince is the thief," said Tracy.

"Impossible," said Angie.

"Prince is big enough to carry a skateboard away in his mouth," said Tracy.

"Why?" said Angie.

"Jealousy," suggested Tracy. "Have you been playing with Prince enough lately?"

"Let's start looking," said Angie.

The girls searched in every room—under beds, sofas, and tables. They couldn't find the skateboard.

"You shouldn't have jumped to conclusions and accused Prince," said Angie. She went to the back door and whistled. Prince came running inside.

"I must go before it's dark," said Tracy. "Perhaps while I'm walking home I will be able to put the clues together better and come up with another lead."

Just then Prince caught sight of some birds walking across the lawn. Barking loudly, he pushed his front paws against the back screen door. The door swung open. Prince went chasing after the birds.

"That's it," said Tracy. "Prince went to your bedroom while you were bathing, picked your skateboard up in his mouth, went to the back door, pushed it open, then went outside and buried it."

"He doesn't even bury bones. He eats them completely!"

"Let's look anyhow," said Tracy.

The girls hunted through the yard. Suddenly Tracy yelled, "Come quick, Angie."

Half-buried in a slope of daisies were dozens of old bones and one brown skateboard with black grip tape.

Angie let out a yell of delight that sounded like "Skateboard World, here I come." She picked up her skateboard.

Prince ran to her side and began barking. "OK, I'll play with you," said Angie.

"Teach Prince a new trick—like how to ride a skateboard," said Tracy.

Angie laughed. "Not a bad idea. He's a real smart dog."

Tracy opened her notebook and wrote *Case solved. P.S. Be on lookout for dog riding skateboard.*

The Clue in the Zoo

By Herma Silverstein

"Let's go see the lions first," said Larry as he and Susan got to the zoo.

"OK," she agreed.

Larry watched his favorite lion pace between the jungle trees. "Hi, lion," said Larry.

"Will you roar for us today?" asked Susan.

The golden lion stopped pacing and opened his mouth wide.

Larry waited to hear the thunderous roar. But the lion merely yawned.

Suddenly, "Help me!" a child's voice cried.

Larry blinked. Susan gasped.

"Did you hear that?" she shouted. "The lion talked."

"Don't be silly. Lions can't talk," Larry said.

"Help me!" the voice cried again. "Get the leash!"

"A leash," repeated Susan. "Why would the lion want a leash?"

Larry glanced behind him at the bears' habitat. Some people were watching a polar bear sit on its hind legs. But Larry and Susan were the only people watching the lions.

"Help! Help!" the voice cried.

"It sounds like a little boy," said Larry.

"Let's find him," said Susan. "He needs help."

Larry peered at the lions' habitat. He saw lions —but no little boy who needed help.

Susan checked the monkeys' island next door. She saw monkeys—but no little boy who needed help.

"Help me!" came the voice again. "Here's your change!"

"What change?" asked Susan. Larry spun around. "The voice is coming from the elephants. Hurry!"

"Help me!" the voice cried. "Closing time, Sam."

"It's not closing time," Susan shouted. "And my name's not Sam." She ran after Larry.

"Where are you?" Larry hollered to the voice.

"By the kitten!" came the reply.

"What kitten?" asked Susan. "All I see are elephants and palm trees."

Larry saw Mr. Jolly, the zookeeper, pushing a wheelbarrow. "Mr. Jolly, come quick! A little boy's trapped in the zoo. But we can't find him."

The zookeeper looked around. "I don't see anyone," he said.

"But we heard him," Susan insisted. "We have to help him."

"Help me!" the voice cried as if answering Susan. "Feed the fish!"

"That's him," Susan exclaimed. "But what fish live with the elephant?"

Suddenly one of the elephants stomped its feet, reared its trunk up, and trumpeted at a palm tree.

Larry looked way up into the tree. A black bird with a yellow beak was perched at the very top of the palm tree.

"There's your mystery voice," Larry shouted.

"It's a myna bird!" Susan cried. "How did it get out of the birdhouse?"

Mr. Jolly shook his head. "Our zoo doesn't own a myna bird."

"Then whose is it?" asked Susan.

"I don't know," answered Mr. Jolly. He rubbed his chin, thinking. "That bird said, 'Feed the fish.' Myna birds imitate people's voices, but they don't know what the words mean."

Larry frowned. "Maybe the myna bird is imitating its owner. It could be giving us clues."

Susan's eyes widened. "The bird said, 'Get the leash.'"

Larry nodded. "It said, 'Here's your change,' and 'By the kitten.'" He thought a minute.

"Those are strange clues," said Mr. Jolly.

Susan frowned. "We know the owner has a dog, some fish, a kitten, and gives out change."

"Change," Larry repeated. A wide grin crept across his face. "This bird's owner also owns something else," he said.

"What?" asked Mr. Jolly.

"A pet store," announced Larry.

"How did you figure that out?" asked Susan.

"'Here's your change' made me think that people have to buy something to get change."

Susan laughed. "'By the kitten.' The myna bird didn't mean *b-y* the kitten. It meant *b-u-y* the kitten."

Larry beamed. "Exactly. The only problem is finding the right pet store."

"You forgot one clue," said Susan. "This myna bird belongs to Sam's Pet Store!"

Larry snapped his fingers. "You're right. I'd forgotten that last clue— 'Closing time, Sam.'"

They went with Mr. Jolly to phone the pet store. When Sam, the owner, arrived, he carried a leash in one hand and a big box in the other. He whistled toward the palm tree. The myna bird flew down and landed on Sam's shoulder. Sam quickly fastened the leash to the bird's collar.

"Thank you for finding Mindy," said Sam. "She flew away while I was cleaning her cage." Sam opened the big box. He pulled out two plastic cages. "These are for you and Larry."

"Hermit crabs!" shouted Larry and Susan. "Thank you."

Susan held her crab by its crusty shell. "I'll name my hermit crab Myna, after Sam's myna bird."

Larry felt the crab's claws walk over his hand. "I'll name mine Mystery."

"What's the mystery?" asked Sam.

Larry laughed as the crab tickled his palm. "Susan and I solved the mystery of the myna bird together. Our crabs' names should go together, too. So we'll always have a Myna Mystery."

Mr. Jolly and Sam laughed with Larry, Susan, and Mindy, the Myna Mystery Bird.

The Midnight Mystery

By Brenda Marshall Bortz

Jackson just couldn't believe it. Except for the old desk and cot, the room was empty. His mother was shaking her head.

"Honey, that cat of yours is gone."

Jackson sat down on the cot slowly. But the funny little squeak didn't make him smile. Two weeks ago he had found a hungry black kitten near the railroad tracks. He had named it Midnight, and his mother had said he could keep it. He still remembered that moment.

"Why not?" she had said. "We won't be living on the second floor much longer. You'll have a yard to play in."

Jackson had giggled. Maybe Midnight would have his own tree to climb! But all that was over now.

This morning his Uncle Steve and Grandpa came early with the moving truck. And the boy put Midnight in the spare room so he'd be safe.

He was careful to close the window and the door. Yet the kitten had got out. The dish of milk on the floor was untouched. Jackson's mother was thinking hard.

"Your Uncle or Grandpa must have opened this door, Jackson. I know they told you they didn't, but maybe they forgot."

Jackson looked up at her. "Then Midnight must have followed us outside when we weren't looking."

Without another word, he jumped up and ran out of the empty apartment and down the stairs. The door to the street was still open.

It was a cold, windy Saturday and scraps of paper were tumbling on the sidewalk. But no kitten was chasing them. As usual, cars were parked all along the curb.

Jackson looked under four or five of them. No luck.

"Hey, what's up?" said a voice. Jackson looked up to see Ricky Sanchez, his best friend.

"I'm looking for Midnight. He got out some-how." Ricky looked worried.

"We've got to find him, Jackson. He's too little to be loose."

Together the boys covered the block. They rattled garbage cans, looked in store windows, and even rang doorbells.

But no one had seen a small black kitten.

When darkness came, the two friends gave up. With a lump in his throat, Jackson said good-bye to Ricky. He probably wouldn't see him for a long time.

Then he went home. When his mother heard the door close, she called out from the kitchen. But Jackson didn't answer.

He went to his room and closed the door. Then he threw himself on the bed. How could he leave here tomorrow? If he did, no one would be around if Midnight came back.

After a while Jackson heard voices in the kitchen. His grandparents had come to say good-bye. All of a sudden his grandpa's deep voice got louder.

"Barbara, you move tomorrow—cat or no cat! That job won't wait. And Jackson's due in his new school Monday."

Jackson pressed his lips together and turned his face to the wall. He wouldn't go. He wouldn't!

Finally, he drifted off to sleep. The next thing he knew, the hall light was shining in his eyes.

His grandmother was a shadow in the doorway.

"Jackson."

He heard her soft voice, but he pretended he was asleep.

"Since your daddy died, your mamma has been working hard—standing on her feet in a store all day and studying nights to get a better job. Tomorrow you can help her, or you can make it hard. It's up to you."

The door closed again, and Jackson looked into the dark for a long time. The next morning he slept late. When he went to the kitchen he saw his mother in the living room. She was tying boxes, and he hurried past.

When he came back from the kitchen, his mother stopped him. She was looking hard at the knot she was tying.

"Jackson," she said, "would you like to say good-bye to Ricky before we go?"

He listened to his voice answer. It sounded far away.

"I already said good-bye, Mother. I—I guess I'd better help you."

She looked up at him and smiled.

"You know, Jackson, you look a lot like your daddy right now."

Working together, they packed the last odds and ends. Then it was time to check the apartment one last time. Jackson opened the door to the spare room and looked around.

The cot and desk were supposed to stay, so everything looked all right. But then Jackson saw the dish of cat food.

It was in the same place as yesterday, but it looked different. Jackson wrinkled his nose as he thought. And then he had it. The dish was half-empty!

He peered under the squeaky cot. Nothing. Then he turned to the old desk. But the drawers were just as empty as they were yesterday.

Suddenly Jackson got an idea. He lifted out the big center drawer. It wasn't nearly as deep as the desk was. As he reached toward the extra space in back, he heard a little purr. It was Midnight, safe and comfortable in his hideout.

Jackson lifted him out and held him against his chest for a while. When he looked up, he saw his mother in the doorway.

"Midnight was here all the time!" Jackson said excitedly. "The noise must have scared him, and he crawled up inside the desk."

His mother was puzzled.

"But how did you know he was there?" she asked.

Jackson grinned so hard his ears moved.

"That was easy," he answered. "He ate some food last night."

"You're some detective, Jackson." His mother

began to laugh heartily.

But Jackson was looking down at Midnight. The little cat was sitting on his master's foot. Ignoring both of them, he was washing his face for moving day.

The Elm Avenue Mystery

By Jane K. Priewe

Jan sat on her front-porch steps with her best friend, staring at large, lopsided *B*'s, *P*'s, and *S*'s chalked on the walks. Overnight, the mysterious letters had appeared in front of almost every house on Elm Avenue.

"Who do you think the chalker is, Meg?"

Meg shrugged. "I want to know why there's an *S* on my walk and a *B* on yours."

Jan pondered the Elm Avenue mystery for a minute. "What do you suppose those letters stand for?"

"Search me! This morning I saw Mr. Tullen looking around. He winked at me and pointed to the walk. Jan! You suppose he . . ."

"No. There's a *P* on his walk. He wouldn't mess up his own place, would he?"

"Guess not," Meg agreed. "What about Mrs. Simms? A couple of weeks ago she turned Mr. Little's rainwater barrel over because she said it was drawing mosquitoes. There's no letter on her sidewalk."

"Aw, come on, Meg! How could she be sour on almost everyone for blocks? Besides, when Mrs. Simms has a complaint, she tells you to your face."

"Dick Stone? He's always in trouble at school, Jan, and we saw him yesterday afternoon."

"Messing with chalk is too tame for Dick. He'd dream up something a lot worse than that."

"Well, whoever did it sure has shaken up the neighborhood. Mr. Boyer called the police and complained."

"So did Mrs. Simms." Jan grinned. "I bet she complained louder than Mr. Boyer."

Jan leaned forward to peer down the street. A small bike with training wheels, heavily loaded with newspapers, wobbled a crisscross pattern from one side of the street to the other.

"Isn't that Theodore Turner?"

"Yes. He's our new paper carrier," Meg answered.

"He looks too little to be hauling that load." Jan felt sorry for the boy.

Jan watched Theodore toss a paper onto Mr. Tullen's porch before he rode back across the street. He climbed the steps to Meg's front door and placed a paper behind the screen door. The little boy waved as he passed, continuing his zigzag course down Elm Avenue.

A week later tongues still wagged over the mysterious letters. People washed the chalk off, but messy *B*'s, *P*'s, and *S*'s were always back the next morning. Jan wished she could discover who was doing it because some of the neighbors were beginning to act suspicious of Meg and her.

"I've heard so many crazy ideas of how they get here," she said one evening as she and Meg returned from an errand to the corner store. "Wouldn't surprise me if little green people from Mars were doing it."

Meg yanked Jan from under a streetlight and pointed toward someone kneeling by the walk halfway down the block. "Maybe it's the chalker!" she whispered.

Walking on grass to muffle their footsteps, they crept closer. A bucket clattered and water splashed. The figure stood and trudged past a driveway.

"Who is it, Jan?"

"Can't tell. Let's get closer."

When a twig snapped under Jan's foot, the figure looked up. It was Theodore Turner.

"Hey, what are you doing?" Meg asked.

"Washing these letters off the sidewalk. I'm finished with them."

Jan chuckled. "So *you're* the chalker! You've had the neighborhood in a purple tizzy for a week!"

"I kind of figured I did. I had to put most of the marks back every evening."

"Why did you put them there in the first place?" Meg asked.

"The newspaper only gave me my job on trial. They thought I was too young." Theodore stood and said proudly, "I *proved* I could do it. Now I'm a regular!"

Jan followed Meg and the little boy to the next chalked letter. "What did they stand for, the letters?"

"I asked all my customers where they wanted me to put their papers. Some wanted them behind their screen doors, so I made an *S*." He aimed a grin at Jan. "Your folks want their paper at the back door, so I put a *B* on your curb. *P* stands for porch."

Meg chuckled. "Boy, Theodore, that's smart thinking."

He nodded and scrubbed harder. "Now that I've learned my route, I don't need the letters anymore," he said, smiling.

"Want some help?" Jan looked at Meg, and Meg nodded.

"Well, sure."

"We'll let our folks know we're back from the store first," Meg said. "Won't they be surprised when we tell them we're helping the mysterious chalker clean sidewalks?"

Jan laughed. "And who the chalker is! I'm almost sorry the mystery's solved. I was hoping it *would* be Martians."

Small Fry's Discovery

By Marlene E. Bomgardner

Mr. Spudster was a lonely potato farmer. He grew a few beans and a few carrots. But mostly he grew potatoes. He just loved potatoes.

Mr. Spudster ate potatoes cooked or raw. He ate them whole or mashed. He ate them diced or french fried. Nobody loved potatoes as much as Mr. Spudster loved potatoes. But there was nobody to eat potatoes with him.

Then a summer came that was very, very hot. The sun was too warm. The wind blew too often. And the rain came not at all. Mr. Spudster's potatoes didn't grow. Well, they grew a little. Very little. Little as marbles. Mr. Spudster worried that he wouldn't have potatoes to last the whole snowy winter. And he just loved potatoes.

When the potatoes were all dug, there was just one bushel of potatoes, small as marbles. Mr. Spudster was sure they would not last the whole snowy winter. Now what would he do?

The cold snows came. The winter winds blew. And it was so cold that icicles hung from the roof of Mr. Spudster's house all day without melting a drop.

One extracold night Mr. Spudster heard a feeble *thump-thump* at his door. He thought he was dreaming, so he didn't get out of bed to see what it was.

In the morning when the cold winter sun shone through his window, he remembered hearing the feeble *thump-thump* and opened his door a crack to peek. There was a little dog curled into a tight ball of black fur. It was so cold that the ball of fur could hardly unroll. The little dog's eyes looked cold and sad. His tail drooped and shivered.

Mr. Spudster took him into his warm kitchen. Soon the little dog thawed into a soft, cuddly ball of fur. His eyes were a warm, excited brown, and his tail wagged happily. Mr. Spudster shared some of his breakfast. It was potatoes. Now Mr. Spudster wasn't the only one who liked potatoes. He named his dog Small Fry, because they both just loved potatoes.

Mr. Spudster was not so lonely now. But the potatoes! They became fewer and fewer. One day when Mr. Spudster started to make supper, he reached into the bushel basket. His hand touched the bottom. Next, Mr. Spudster tipped the bushel basket upside down, but no potatoes rolled out. Small Fry barked. He seemed to know there was trouble. That night Mr. Spudster and Small Fry went to bed hungry. Hungry for potatoes.

For many days Mr. Spudster and Small Fry had to settle for a few beans and a few carrots. Oh, how they missed those potatoes. They loved potatoes more than absolutely anything.

One night a quiet shadow moved across the fields to Mr. Spudster's house. Small Fry barked. Mr. Spudster paid no attention to the shadow because nobody ever came to his house. Ever.

But this time someone did, and Small Fry barked so loudly that Mr. Spudster finally opened the door. There was a bushel basket of potatoes. Now they had potatoes to eat again. Oh, how they loved those wonderful potatoes!

A few days later, Mr. Spudster went to the little shed behind his house to prepare his tools for spring so he could plant more potatoes. He found tracks in the snow. Old tracks. Small Fry sniffed the tracks, then followed them across the field. Mr. Spudster called, "Small Fry, come back!"

But the little dog wouldn't. Mr. Spudster had no choice but to follow.

The tracks led to a house on the edge of town. The house had a little shed behind it, too. The tracks led right up to the shed. Small Fry scratched at the door. Out came a man with a hoe in his hand. He was mending the handle and oiling the metal. Mr. Spudster knew this was how you prepared tools for spring so you could plant potatoes. Maybe he'd found someone else who loved potatoes.

Shyly, Mr. Spudster said, "Hello."

The man answered, "Hello! I'm Mr. Taters. And you must be Mr. Spudster."

Mr. Taters invited them into his big, homey kitchen to meet Mrs. Taters and their eight children. Soon they learned that they all loved potatoes. Mr. Spudster found out where his bushel of potatoes had come from on that dark winter night. The townspeople had each given a few potatoes until there was a bushel, and Mr. Taters was the someone who had taken the basket to Mr. Spudster's door. Mr. Spudster thanked Mr. Taters heartily, and they all became friends.

Mr. Spudster is still a potato farmer. But he's not lonely anymore. He has Small Fry and his new friends, the Taters family, near town. And they all just love potatoes.

The Red Purse Mystery

By Ann Bixby Herold

The vending machines were in an open-fronted shelter near the beach.

Aaron and Anne checked the shelter at least once a day. People often dropped coins on the sandy floor.

It was a hot summer afternoon.

"Thirsty weather," Aaron called it.

This time they were lucky. Under the machines Anne found a quarter. Aaron found two dimes.

"Orange," said Aaron.

"Cola," Anne said.

They decided the way they always did. The person who found the most money made the choice.

There was a patch of shade behind the shelter. They sat with their backs against the wooden planks and shared the cold drink. They listened as a family entered the shelter. A woman's voice was counting out change. A baby started to cry.

Aaron put his eye to a crack in the planking.

"Did they drop any coins?" Anne asked when they had gone. She was hungry.

"I don't see any. Hey! The mother left her purse." He shifted to get a better look. "A red one."

There was another crack higher up. Anne squinted through it.

"I see it. We'd better return it. Would you recognize the family?"

"Sure. One small kid. One baby in a stroller. The mother was wearing red shorts and red sandals. The dad . . ."

"Wait," Anne said. "I hear voices."

Two teenage girls entered the shelter. As one girl fed coins into the soda machine, the other picked up the purse. She opened it, took out the wallet, and looked inside. With a smile she dropped the purse into a straw beach bag.

"Let's go," said the girl.

"They stole it!" Aaron said when the girls had gone.

"You don't know that," Anne argued. "Maybe the mother sent them back for it."

"They weren't with the lady before. Besides, I didn't like the way that girl smiled when she looked in the wallet."

"Oh, Aaron. She was just checking to see if the money was there."

"I don't think so. I'm going to follow them."

"Why?"

"I don't know. Just a hunch. If you don't want to come, don't."

When Aaron ran after the girls, Anne was right behind him.

"You'll look stupid if they're taking it to the police," she panted.

"Shhh!" he hissed.

The two girls were up ahead. One was swinging the beach bag. They were talking and laughing as they sipped their sodas. They walked right past a police officer.

"They aren't acting guilty," Anne whispered. "Maybe they *are* the woman's kids. Do you see her anywhere?"

Aaron shook his head.

A crowd had gathered near the entrance to the amusement pier. A mime group was putting on a show. The girls had stopped to watch.

"You watch them," Aaron whispered. "I'll scout around for the family."

When he had gone, Anne edged closer. Her heart was beating fast. She listened, but neither of the girls said anything. When Aaron came back and beckoned to her, he looked pleased.

"I found the family. See that woman in red shorts sitting on the wall over there? Next to the man holding a baby? That's her. She isn't acting as if she lost her purse. Maybe she doesn't know it's missing."

"Maybe it isn't her purse."

"Of course it is! I saw her put it down when she picked up her baby. Did you get a peek into the beach bag?"

"I tried. All I could see was a towel. If the purse is in there, it doesn't mean it's stolen," Anne argued. "I bet they are her kids."

"Then why haven't they told her they found the purse?" Aaron demanded. "They haven't been anywhere near her. I bet they stole it."

"OK. I give up," Anne sighed. "They stole it! Now what are we going to do about it?"

"I don't know. Keep watch, I guess. You stick with the two girls. I'll be over by the family."

Nothing happened until the show was over, and the parents started to collect their children. The woman jumped up and screamed. "My purse! It's gone. Somebody stole my purse!"

The baby started to cry. The husband glared. The people closest to them backed away, as if they were afraid of being blamed.

To his surprise, Aaron heard himself say, "You

74

left it by the soda machine."

"I did? Oh, I remember. I'm sorry I got so excited."

"Where is it?" her husband asked.

Everyone was staring at Aaron. His brain seemed to freeze, yet his face was burning hot.

"I—I—" he stuttered.

"I found it," a voice said.

Anne pushed her way through the crowd. She was holding the red purse.

The woman thanked them. The man gave them a dollar. Anne said they couldn't take it, but the man absolutely insisted.

Aaron could hardly wait until everyone had gone.

"How did you get the purse?" he asked.

Anne smiled mysteriously. "I'm sorry, I can't . . . Great spies never give away their secrets."

Aaron grabbed her arm. "Tell me! *Please!*"

"When the woman screamed, those girls looked so guilty! They edged out of the crowd, and I followed them. No one else saw them go. Everyone was staring at the lady. I saw them toss the purse into a trash can and run down the beach."

"Did they take the wallet out?"

"They didn't have time. As soon as they left, I fished the purse out." She grinned and waved the dollar. "I'm hungry, Aaron."

"Me, too. My choice this time?"

The Great Samsoni

By Elizabeth L. Zorc

The Great Samsoni—that's me. My real name is Sam, of course, but I'm trying out names for my stage career as a magician.

"The Great Samsoni," I announced at the dinner table.

"Samsoni Baloney! Pass the peas," my sister Louise said. I imagined what she would look like with peas growing out of her head instead of blonde hair. I tried to make the peas move by mental telepathy, but they just sat there.

This year I'm going to be in the fifth-grade talent show, and I've been trying to come up with a big finish for my act. I was thinking this over the next day as I walked home from school. I had my deck of magic cards with me, and I just strolled along, shuffling them as I went. Maybe I could pull a rabbit out of a hat? Well, we don't have a rabbit, and the only other animal in the house is her pet hamster.

About then I noticed I was passing Greenville Academy. There was a kid walking out of the gate. Two men were waiting for him by a black car. Something just didn't seem right. One man got on each side of the boy and sort of helped him into the car. Maybe I imagined it, but the kid really seemed scared. He didn't look too happy about going with them.

The hairs on the back of my neck were sort of tickling, so I stepped behind a bush where the men couldn't see me. I thought I should at least get the license number of the car—5QAJ862. I had my cards in my hand, so I quickly pulled out a five, a queen, an ace, a jack, an eight, a six, and a two. Then I stacked the cards on top of the deck in that order as the car pulled away.

As I walked the rest of the way home, I sort of forgot about the whole thing. I was more worried about how I could get Louise to let me use her hamster in my magic act.

Louise decided to charge me a dime per rehearsal and a quarter for the performance to use her precious pet. The next night I was busy using my first dime's worth of hamster when something on television caught my eye. There was the boy I'd seen outside the Academy, and the announcer was saying he was missing!

For a minute I was kind of stunned while my brain turned things over. Then I told my parents.

Well, we called the police, and a detective came over to talk to me. I felt kind of important, especially when I said I knew the license number. I pulled out my cards and laid out the first seven. My dad said this was no time to do a card trick, but I explained the cards meant 5QAJ862.

Now I was pretty worried. What if I had waited too long to call the police? What if the little boy was in real trouble because of me? I stayed by the phone and hoped for someone to call, and I worried.

At last! The boy was found! The detective said the license number helped crack the case. I felt great.

"Wow," Louise said, "you really do know magic." She was so impressed she let me use the hamster for free.

Mystery Morning

By Rebecca Horst

Jennifer, Julie, and Jackie Jones had played every game in the house twice. Their stack of library books had dwindled. The two younger girls were off somewhere with their noses stuck in the last of the mysteries, but Jennifer closed her book with a thump. "I'm tired of this old winter vacation," she complained to her mom. "I wish some *real* mysteries would happen around here."

"Well," suggested Mother, "maybe you'll just have to create some." She gave Jennifer a pat on the bottom and said, "Now, scoot. I want to work on my needlepoint."

Jennifer stood still for an instant. Then her eyes began to twinkle. "Hey, Julie, Jackie, come here," she yelled, rushing out of the room. "I've got an idea!"

Next door Mr. Slemmer slowly pulled on his coat and boots as the three girls watched. Mrs. Slemmer, who warned him to be careful, was always saying he would have a heart attack.

"But I have to shovel the walk," he explained. "It's a city ordinance. I'll be all right."

The girls giggled as he fetched the snow shovel from the garage. But when he came around to the front door, his eyes widened in surprise. "Why, come and look, Edith," he gasped. "It's already done."

"Whoever did it dropped a red mitten," observed Mrs. Slemmer, whose eyes must have been sharper than her husband's. "And look at those footprints. Don't they come from next door?"

Across the street Mrs. Baum was jiggling a hungry baby on her hip while trying to take her toddler's temperature. Through the kitchen window, Jennifer, Julie, and Jackie could see last night's supper dishes still piled in the sink.

The girls rang the doorbell and hid.

"Just what I need," Mrs. Baum said, making her way to the door. But no one was there. Just a covered basket and a blue mitten that some-one had dropped.

She peeked under the basket's cover and found a plate of cookies, some slightly used coloring books, a new box of crayons, and a small clown doll. Her baby cooed and reached for the clown. Mrs. Baum smiled.

"I know I've seen that clown doll before," she said as she picked up the basket. "Wasn't it when the girls across the street baby-sat for me last month?"

Looking in the bay window of the house at the corner, the girls saw Miss Kratz take her daily dose of aspirin for her arthritis. Most of her days were spent in a rocking chair beside the big window. Jennifer, Julie, and Jackie hid as Miss Kratz settled in her rocking chair. Then she stared in amazement.

The tree outside her window was hopping with activity. A pair of cardinals, three purple finches, several juncos, and a dozen or so sparrows and chickadees were all crowding around the bird feeder that most certainly had not been there yesterday. On the ground under the tree was one green mitten.

Miss Kratz smiled.

From their hiding place behind the frosty yew hedge, the three girls smiled, too.

Miss Kratz seemed to think for a minute, then

she went to the phone.

Mother passed the door to the cellar and looked in to investigate. Three happy faces looked up. "Aren't you ready for lunch, girls?" she asked. "It's past one o'clock."

"In a little bit, Mom. We're sorting the nails and screws and cleaning up the scrap wood-pile," explained Jennifer. "Please don't tell Dad we did it."

"We want it to be a secret," Julie added.

Mother arched her eyebrows and put her finger to her lips. "I'll never tell," she whispered to the girls. "By the way," she added, "do you girls know where all the cookies you made yesterday went to?"

Before the girls could answer, the doorbell rang. The girls followed Mother to the door.

There stood Mrs. Baum from across the street with a happy baby and a blue mitten.

Beside her was Mr. Slemmer from next door holding out red and green mittens. "I believe these belong to you girls," he said, smiling. "You've been mighty busy this morning. I want to thank you for shoveling my walk, and Miss Kratz is just tickled pink with her new bird feeder."

"And I want to thank you girls, too," broke in Mrs. Baum. "The cookies and toys you left were just what the children and I needed to cheer up our day."

"But I don't understand," began Mother. She glanced back into the kitchen and noticed for the first time that the table had been set for lunch. The sandwiches were already made. Beyond the table, resting on the radiator to dry, were one red, one blue, and one green mitten.

Jennifer, Julie, and Jackie giggled.

"Are you sure it was us?" asked Jackie.

"It could have been anyone," said Julie.

"It could be a real mystery!" said Jennifer.

"It could be," said Mother.

The Valentine Mystery

By Shirley Markham Jorjorian

Benny counted his valentines again. "Twenty-nine," he said. "That's all—one from each class-mate and one from Miss Williams." But then he heard Miss Williams say, "Benny Bernard—another one for you."

How could it be? Benny thought. I already have one from everybody!

He walked slowly to the front, trying to figure if he had counted wrong. He looked to see who had sent the valentine. It was a plain red hand-made one. In large awkward print, it read "Be My Valentine—Guess Who."

"I wonder who sent it. Could it be one of the girls? Maybe it's Ann who's always staring at me. No, that couldn't be. She gave me one with her name on it. And who would want to give me two valentines? Oh, it must be a joke one of the guys is playing on me."

Benny examined the printing for clues. All the *N*'s were printed backwards. Whoever it was either couldn't print well, or part of the joke was to print the *N*'s backwards to mislead him.

Just then Benny heard his name again. Miss Williams called him to the front. "Benny," she said, "there are only four valentines left in the box, and it seems they're all for you."

He hurried to the front, more puzzled than ever. He returned to his desk and stared at the valentines. They all had the backwards *N*'s and were signed "Guess Who" like the first one. This is going to take some detective work, thought Benny, but I'm going to find out who "Guess Who" is.

Days went by and Benny had no more clues than he started with—just the backwards *N*'s. "If I could get everyone to print my name, maybe that would tell who gave me the valentines. But how could I get everyone in the class to print it without the guilty one knowing why I was doing it? Oh, I've got an idea—an autograph book!"

Next day Benny had all his classmates write in his autograph book, making sure they printed "To Benny" so he could check to see how each one made the *N*'s. He studied them carefully during lunch. No one printed the *N*'s backwards.

Well, I guess I'll have to start all over, looking for some other clue, he thought. Wish I had someone to help me, but I don't dare say anything about it to anyone. I might be telling the very one who gave me the valentines.

Just then Benny looked around. There was no one else in the lunchroom. "Oh, no. I must have been thinking so hard I didn't hear the bell. I'm late for math class, and I have to get my books from the locker."

He rushed to the locker, grabbed a stack of books, and ran to math class. He sat down and flipped open his book. Then he realized he'd grabbed his little brother's third-grade math book instead of his own. He and Chuck shared the same locker. He stared at the name printed in large and awkward letters—Chuck Bernard. And the *N* in Bernard was printed backwards! It was the same printing that was on his valentines.

But why? thought Benny. Why would Chuck want to give me five valentines?

When school was out, Benny went to meet Chuck to walk home with him.

"Hi, Chuck. I want to ask you something. Did you put five valentines signed 'Guess Who' in my homeroom box on Valentine's Day?" questioned Benny.

"Well, uh, uh, yes," stammered Chuck.

"But why, Chuck? I don't understand," said Benny.

"Well, just before Valentine's Day, I had a terrible dream that you didn't get any valentines at all and that all the kids laughed at you. I wanted to make sure you got some cards from your friends."

"Chuck," said Benny happily, "you're a terrific brother and the best friend I have. After all, the other kids just gave me one valentine and you gave me *five.*"

Who Owns This Dog?

By Mary L. Lovett

Terry and his parents had just moved into a big house in the country when the brown-and-white dog came to live with them. He was standing at the kitchen door one morning when Terry came to breakfast. The moment they met, they knew they belonged together.

"May I keep him?" Terry asked his parents. "We have plenty of room, and I promise to do everything for him myself."

The dog's eyes seemed to be begging Terry's parents to let him stay. Terry's eyes were pleading, too. All his life he had wanted a dog. He didn't really care what kind. A big dog, little dog, or any kind of dog would do, just as long as it belonged to him. Always before they had lived in an apartment in the city where dogs weren't allowed; but now they had plenty of room and a dog that really wanted to belong to him.

"I'm sure a nice dog like that already belongs to someone," his mother said.

"But he came to me," Terry pleaded, "and you can see he wants to stay."

His father patted the dog on the head. "Of course he'd like to stay," he said. "But if he belongs to someone else, he must be returned."

"We could put an ad in the paper," Terry said and wondered to himself if there was any way the ad could be worded to describe the dog so people wouldn't recognize him, and still tell the truth.

"There's a much quicker way," his father said. "Take the dog to town today and try to find his real owner. If he is not claimed, you may keep him."

On his way to town, Terry thought hard. Maybe if he just walked around in town and looked at the displays in the store windows, people wouldn't ask questions.

But he knew that wasn't what his father meant. He really had to try to find the dog's owner.

"But I'll find a way to keep you," he promised the dog. "You just leave everything to me."

When he reached town, he stopped in front

of Atkins' Grocery Store and patted the dog's head reassuringly. Just then three boys, who had been watching from across the street, came over to join him.

"I haven't seen you around before," the largest of the three boys said. "What's your name?"

"Terry Willis. I live in the yellow house down the road," Terry explained. "We just moved here from Chicago."

"You have a nice dog," the smallest boy said. "What do you call him?"

Terry thought of a name, then changed his mind.

"He just walked into our kitchen this morning," he explained, "but my father says I can keep him if no one claims him today."

The largest boy put his hands in his pockets and looked at the dog.

"He's mine, of course," he said. "I'd know him anywhere by his brown ears."

The middle-sized boy moved closer to get a better look.

"Your dog might have had brown ears," he said, "but mine had a brown front paw, like this one. He's my dog."

"You're both wrong," the smallest boy told them. "He's my dog. Look how he wags his tail when he hears my voice."

Terry was confused. He hadn't planned on a problem like this.

"He can't belong to all of you," he told the boys, "and I'm not giving him up without better proof of ownership."

The three boys started arguing among themselves. They talked so loud they didn't hear Mr. Atkins come to the door of his store until he cleared his throat to attract their attention.

"I want to see the owner of that dog," he announced. "I've been feeding him from my store for almost a month."

Without waiting for an answer, he stalked back into his store, leaving four surprised boys staring after him.

"Do you think he wants someone to pay for feeding that dog?" the middle-sized boy asked.

The largest boy looked at the dog again. "He does have a brown front paw!" he exclaimed. "You're right. He's not my dog."

The middle-sized boy got down on his knees to examine the dog's paws. "I thought there was something different about this dog," he explained. "His right foot is brown. My dog's brown paw was on the left side. He's not my dog."

"He couldn't be mine either," the smallest boy said. "I've been watching him, and I can see now that it's Terry he's looking at when he wags his tail."

The three boys hurried off down the street.

"I guess you're my dog, all right," Terry told

his new friend, "but before we go home, we'll have to work something out with Mr. Atkins."

Mr. Atkins smiled when Terry and the dog entered the store. "I see they left you with the dog," he said, and this time he didn't sound at all gruff.

"I can't pay you for feeding him," Terry said, "but I can work. I could clean your store and run errands for you every day."

Mr. Atkins laughed. "You have paid already," he said. "You have shown me that you want the dog enough to be willing to make a sacrifice to keep him."

"I'll take good care of him, too," Terry promised, "and I'll bring him to see you every time we come to town."

The dog seemed to know everything had been settled. He barked impatiently and started toward his new home with Terry following close behind him.